Life, After All

Other Books by Suzanne Jacob:

Flore Cocon, novel, (Montréal: Parti pris, 1978)

Poèmes I: Gémellaires, le Chemin de Damas, poetry, (Montréal: le biocreux, 1980)

Laura Laur, novel, (Paris: Seuil, 1983)

La passion selon Galatée, novel, (Paris: Seuil, 1986)

Les aventures de Pomme Douly, short stories, (Montréal: Boréal, 1988)

Maude, novel, (Montréal: NBJ, 1988)

Life, After All

Suzanne Jacob

TRANSLATED BY SUSANNA FINNELL

PRESS GANG PUBLISHERS

VANCOUVER

Canadian Cataloguing in Publication Data
  Jacob, Suzanne
    [La survie. English]
    Life, after all

  Translation of: La survie.
  ISBN 0-88974-017-8

  I. Title. II. Title: La survie. English.
  PS8569.A286S9713 1988   C843'.54   C89-091007-3
  PQ3919.2.J32S9713 1988

Portions of this book were previously published as follows: *The Observing
Mind* in *(f.)Lip, a newsletter of feminist innovative writing*, Vol. 2, #4,
March, 1989; an earlier version of *Strawberry Time* in *Ink and Strawberries:
An Anthology of Quebec Women's Fiction*, edited by Beverley Daurio and
Luise von Flotow, translated by Luise von Flotow and Susanna Finnell, Aya
Press, 1988.

First printing, April 1989

Edited by Barbara Kuhne
Production by Val Speidel
Cover design by Carolyn Deby
Type produced by The Typeworks
Printed by the collective labour of Press Gang Printers
Cover printed by Benwell-Atkins Ltd.
Printed and bound in Canada

Press Gang Publishers
603 Powell Street
Vancouver, B.C. V6A 1H2   Canada

Contents

Preface

Life, After All is Suzanne Jacob's first work to appear in English. From her earlier period of writing, it already reflects the major themes of a writer who poses questions of enormous difficulty with great lucidity. Fundamentally the question is about the nature of language, the organization and representation of things in language, and woman's place in this language.

It is a hard-edged, mathematically precise vision softened by the possibility of laughter. The themes appear in simple, exacting stories that fit together like the sharp-cut angles that make a tough diamond appear tougher and clearer in the sum of its parts.

The initial attraction to these stories is their apparent simplicity—and then their inherent resistance, their refusal to lay down and obey the rules. The short pieces of fiction persist and, just like in Marguerite Duras's texts, the experience of reading lingers and really only begins later when the gaps and blanks insidiously insist on participating in the construction of the meaning. It is as if from these blanks some force works up an unseen pattern of seeing something that is not there. That pattern is woman inflected.

From what space does woman inscribe herself onto text? Would it be something like the blank image in the mirror that accompanies *A Woman*? Or more like the doubling of someone who sees herself act as in *For A Navy Blue Sweater*? Do words not belong to *A Little Girl*? And if we were to discard all that is known, all that exists? Will there be life? What would it be? A torn baby buggy—a sign of something yet to come?

These and other questions are delightfully explored in the collection of short fiction pieces that make up *Life, After All*.

—*Susanna Finnell*
April 1989

A Little Girl

A PATIENT LITTLE GIRL who doesn't yet know that there are thousands of other patient little girls is sitting very straight in the brown chair with worn foot rests in the dining room. She doesn't invent anything. She doesn't experiment with words in her mouth. She doesn't think about her birthday, or about the sandboxes with sand finer than the courtyard sand still in her shoes. She doesn't day-dream about the crunchy sound of celery, or about the ant colony going crazy over a bit of hay, or about the smell of bread toasting in the morning while coffee steams from her father's red cup. She doesn't try to imagine a new never-to-be-found hiding place for her secrets. She doesn't hear the sound things make when they come back to take up their place, or the rustling of the three poplars, or the shimmering of summer in the large willow out back that she climbs until she reaches fear. Right now she doesn't feel like running to see if the leaves still taste bitter, or if the grass blades are strong enough to use as whistles between the thumbs.

She doesn't think about the white tablecloth in the sideboard, the one with green flowers that smells of fresh air, or about the cutlery with rose handles, or the box of chocolates put away until next Sunday, or about the light that reaches up the stairs with the voices of the others when she goes to sleep in the evening. She isn't afraid of things that still come out from under the bed to scare her at night.

Right now isn't the time for a nap. Or for a snack, or for dinner. It's time for nothing at all. The quiet little girl sits in the patience of nothingness. She wears time; she waits.

Strawberry Time

I WAS HOLDING THEM in my hands and had to open the door in a complicated way with my elbows and knees, finally kicking it shut. I ran to the kitchen. Our kitchen has a swinging door without handles. I sent it slamming into the green chimney. I'm too loud, my mother always says, my movements are too sweeping, my mouth is too big, I talk too loud, I overflow and that wears her out.

"Mom!"

I looked to see if she was in the yard, sometimes she goes for a breath of air and to look at the trees in the yard. She stands on the porch, looks at the sky and rubs her forehead. She wasn't out there. The bathroom door was closed. I knocked with my elbow because my hands were full.

"Not so loud my God can't you wait a minute?"

Her voice is really something else these days. I'm never quite sure if she is talking or crying, you might say she swallows her words, you are never sure if the words are coming out or going in.

"What's the matter, are you sick?"

It's silly to ask, she is always sick, but then she is never sick. It's her specialty these days and it takes up all her time because she would have to decide once and for all whether or not she is sick and she hates decisions, decisions exhaust her.

"Of course not... my God... you're late. The others have already left again."

"Close your eyes before you come out of the bathroom."

It's obvious that I'm bothering her. If I disturbed her less, she would probably move even less, maybe she would get to the point of not moving at all. At least that's what I've been thinking lately. You could say that there is no movement coming from her anymore, from deep inside. You could say that it's us who keep her alive, my brothers and I, because we need to eat and brush our teeth and go to bed. You could say that these are the only things she is holding onto, you could also say that they are what's holding her together.

I walked around tapping my feet to get on her nerves. I heard water running from the tap. At times she runs the water to wash her hands and then she just stands there listening to it or watching it run. You really have to push her to get her out of it.

"That's enough of it, come on out now!"

"All right... "

She turned off the water.

"Wait! Are your eyes closed? Don't open them until I say so."

My brothers don't notice anything. No one besides me notices because my sisters are in boarding school and besides my sisters there is no one who would really be interested except my father. He notices, but we don't have the same way of noticing. He prefers that those who notice don't talk about it or admit it to each other. That way reactions are freer and there's no need to start a discussion that might turn into an argument and in any case, you don't know the nature of the virus and maybe there is no virus at all.

She was pale, even paler than before, and the brown spots on her forehead and temples stood out and she was rubbing the back of her hand. Her hair was dry and flat like after a bad case of the flu and fever and she doesn't like going to the hairdresser, it's too tiring, it takes all her energy for three days and then three more days to get over it. I wondered for a few seconds if I should go on worrying about her. When I see her like this, I wonder, I tell myself that it might be better to leave her alone. To be still is what she really wants, what she desires, not to eat, or take baths or to get up anymore, ever, at all.

She kept her eyes closed, just as I told her. Maybe she would rather keep them like this because the light hurts her eyes, especially when my father isn't around, when he's away. OK, she was leaning against the fridge.

"You're home late. Marc and Oliver have gone back to school a long time ago. It's one o'clock! You have ten minutes left to eat, your food is going to be cold, it's already cold."

That's all she could say. That was proof of her maternal presence and of the good care she gives me. Eating cold food or eating hot food makes no difference at all to her. Her ideal is to never be hungry again, to not need food in order to live. Ideally, life should be lived through sleep, and sleeping should be all that's needed.

I put my hands under her nose to see if the smell would wake her up even though I knew she wasn't really sleeping, but I feel better when she is really sleeping than when she is leaning against the fridge like this, rubbing the back of her hand, and you can see those brown spots grow bigger around her eyes and on her forehead.

"Don't you smell anything?"

She lifted her head and tried to take three little sniffs of air. It takes all her strength these days. I opened my hands for the smell to reach her switched-off face. That's it, her face is switched off, and you can't figure out anymore how to switch it on, nobody can, nothing works, because she has seen lots of doctors and takes all sorts of medication but she is still not switching on.

But now her nostrils were moving, she swallowed and I saw saliva, just a bit of saliva wetting her lips and they opened a little more and then she opened her eyes and said "Oh."

It worked. It wasn't exactly the greatest "Oh" you could imagine, but for a person going through a difficult time like my mother, it was quite extraordinary.

Usually she has black eyes, for as long as I can remember she had black eyes that shone. Then they stopped shining. It's been about a year. Now, you could say they're fading, but her hair is still very black without any grey strands. She looked at my hands with these faded eyes and I told her to open her mouth, that I was going to give her the solemn communion of the first strawberries of spring from the end of the world—we are far from everything here and the first strawberries come after everyone else has had them according to the paper.

"Don't joke around with these kinds of things my God."

She says this because I said "solemn communion" and she doesn't like it if people make fun of sacred things like communion, being part of religion it must remain sacred because if you can't tell the difference between what's sacred and what's not, what will become of you, you wouldn't know any longer who you owed what to, or who you owed nothing to because debts are sacred too, my father and my mother are in agreement on this, there is a commandment that says to honour them and there is nothing like people who honour their debts, you can trust them forever.

Anyway, I put three strawberries on her tongue, the three reddest, the three largest. Her jaws didn't move, I was watching closely, I was watching to see if her tongue would start moving, but nothing moved and she swallowed.

"You swallow them whole! You could chew them!"

"My God oh no they melt between your tongue and the roof of your mouth."

That's the kind of surprise my mother can give you. You think she's in a coma and then she comes out with something like that, she'll say she likes butter as much as candy or she'll say "Did you notice the form of this apple, Julie?" It seems as if an electric current gets the better of her sleep in moments like that. It makes me sweat, I was sweating, this idea that without a single movement of her muscles, she could notice that the strawberries were melting in her mouth and that made me proud of myself. Then her eyes made a sort of inspection of my hands, blouse, jumper and shoes, all without moving her head, nothing but her eyes, slowly, in one go and she murmured "strawberries... "

There, she was off again. OK. I walked over to the sink, changed my mind and went over to the garbage can, slamming the lid against the wall.

"Not happy?... I'll throw them out."

She moved. She unstuck herself from the fridge and stopped rubbing the back of her hand and opened the cupboard and took out a bowl.

"Don't do that, good God, strawberries... "

"I haven't had any. See, and there isn't a single stem on them."

It was true. I had not eaten a single one. The patch isn't big. When I saw fat Bérubé coming towards me asking if I had found ripe ones, it made me so mad. Every year she thinks that the patch belongs to everybody because it's in a vacant lot and the edges of the roads and ditches are public property. She thinks first-come first-served are just words, she says it every spring each time I find the patch of red berries and it's always me who first thinks of double-checking these kinds of things and just because she lives two steps from us, she thinks she has the same rights to what I see first. *It is my patch*. The Bérubé woman is perfectly useless in a strawberry patch. She doesn't know how to look, she only knows how to squash them with her fat feet, and she only knows how to complain that she can't find anything and how come you find everything and it isn't fair. She really gets on my nerves.

My mother squinted her eyes looking out the window over the sink into the yard. I put the strawberries into the bowl. I washed my hands and dried them on the dish towel. It stained the towel red. My mother saw it and sighed. That's the way it is. When she sighs it means she has enough air in her chest for another breath.

"Your lunch is on the table. I'm going to lie down for a while. I'll keep the strawberries for my snack. Thanks dear, they are splendid, splendid."

I repeated the word to myself. Splendid, splendid. It's the kind of word she uses for strawberries or pebbles she sometimes finds in the yard. It's a word for everything and nothing, a word to toss off for something you don't have, for something that really is missing, even if it might exist.

I wasn't hungry. I looked at my shoes. They are brown Savage shoes, the best for children and adolescents. Monsieur Turgeon who fits us with shoes told my mother that and my mother does not want to buy shoes that are not Savages because Savages are durable too.

I like my shoes. They are scratched just the way I like and really fit my foot without making blisters.

I was late anyway. A little more or less wouldn't matter, I could take my time. It's like when I know there's a mistake in my dictation, I won't correct it. It's all or nothing with me. If

I'm sure there won't be any mistakes, then good, I correct the text. But if I know I will make some mistake anyway because there's a word I can't spell, or a verb I'm not sure about, then, too bad, I won't correct it.

I could hear my mother turning over in her bed even though the door was closed. Before, she used to sing a lot. Now with my brothers at school, it's quiet in our house. Then I hear her crying.

Gerald says that women are made for crying. He says his mother cries about everything, but he and his dad never do. He says crying doesn't help anything.

Because our floor creaks, I was careful not to make any noise as I tip-toed up to the door of their room. It was like I said, I wasn't mistaken, she was crying. She cries funny, my mother. First of all, she is not like Gerald's mother, she doesn't cry for nothing, she doesn't ever cry even though you might think she did now because of her faded eyes and the brown circles around her eyes and on her forehead. She cried once when my sister stepped on a nail and she was the fourth one to step on a nail and that meant work and foot-baths and lotions. It takes a long time to heal feet, it shouldn't, after all you walk with them. But that's the way it is.

That was it all right, she was crying more and more with sobs and sighs. Standing on the other side of the door with one hand on the doorknob, I asked myself what to do. I was thinking that I should hurry back to school, after all I had no business here because I'm usually at school at this time and as far as my mother knew I really was at school.

I turned the knob very carefully so she wouldn't jump, scaring her is not what you want to do to someone who thinks she is alone in the house, especially since our house is rather

21

big and she is crying, assuming that no one can hear her.

I quite like their room. It's the biggest one in the house. They have a big bed with a dark wooden headboard. On one of the walls, the one where the baby bed is, there is wallpaper with white birds on royal blue background. I don't think my mother will have any more babies, I don't know, but she keeps the baby bed in their room just in case. There is a royal blue down cover on their bed. Now, the royal blue down cover, rising and falling, looked as if it was crying.

I don't know what's wrong with her. Something must be wrong. It can happen to anyone, something goes wrong and sometimes it lasts a long time, it's persistent. I know that. But she isn't like everybody. That's my opinion. But what could I do. They each have their dresser and drawers. She reached out towards her dresser and took the whole box of Kleenex with her under the covers. She didn't see me but she could have because of the mirror, she would have jumped, she wouldn't have believed it was me because she doesn't think that I can do anything without making lots of noise or without moving everything including the air.

I don't know, I left their room, I was too hot. I felt my head to see if I had a temperature because I get fevers for no reason at all and my temples were throbbing. If something could make her temples beat like this, I wonder if she would cry, I don't know.

I ran. I straightened my jumper and went to class. Of course she had to make some comment, I can't do anything without her making some comment. If I wanted her to stop making comments, I would have to be like everyone else here and even then she would find a way to prove to herself that I am like everyone else in order to be different. She says I always find a way to be noticed.

"You're late, Miss Chavarie."

That's just like her. That's the way she is, slipping in a comment even if there is no point in disturbing the *whole* class because *one* student comes in late, when it's obvious that everyone has already seen that anyway. But she always has to make a fuss over something or other.

"You're right, Sister, I'm late, excuse me for being late, Sister."

I must have said it in a certain tone. Everyone snickered except Sister and me. There was nothing funny about it but it's true that I said it in a certain way, I agree, she could hold that against me, I'm ready to admit my mistakes when I make them, I admit them most of the time and when I haven't any, I invent them, I invent them even for others if necessary, it doesn't bother me. I opened the top of my desk.

My books and notebooks are all covered with brown wrapping paper, the kind that has a dull side and a shiny side, from the Crépeault grocery store. I wrap my books shiny side out because I think that side is waterproof.

My books were stacked neatly because there had been a general clean-up of our desks since it was close to the Department of Public Instruction examination and that was a good excuse to clean up. An orderly desk is beautiful because the eyes are the mirror of the soul and what is well perceived comes across clearly. With my head in my desk and the lid on my head, I listened to the silence I had produced in the class. There are many qualities of silence, everybody knows that, I knew this particular silence was waiting for me to lower the top of my desk because the open top disturbed the whole class, upset the horizon line that Sister needed in order to concentrate because we were in the review period.

I don't know. It was like I was stuck behind this top. It was like I was paralyzed by this lid that I held up with my head while my hands went through my pencil bag for no reason at all. My desk is in the row by the blackboard because in the row by the windows I get too distracted and talk about what is going on outside and I tell the others what's happening in the school yard and who is going down or coming up Second Street and it drives Sister crazy to hear me talk about the nearby real world. You can only talk about the outside world the way it's told in the books, for and by the books. The School Board's policy is to use textbooks to teach us the colour of the Seine in Paris, its temperature and width and all, and to never talk about the Harricana that cuts right through town here, you cannot talk about that ever ever ever. In any case, this is a colonized country, and that is why you can't ever start out by knowing the names of the trees and bushes and everything and fire-engines are red anyway like everywhere else, it's international and the world is bigger than before, when my mother was born the world was much smaller because the mass media had not, at that point, made the whole planet within reach the way it is now. Anyway, Sister had moved my desk to eliminate the distraction. I'm sure the School Board agrees with this decision and I had no say in it.

"Come on Julie, when are you going to come out of your desk?"

Managing to come out of this desk is just what I wanted most in this internationalized world. She couldn't imagine, and I wasn't going to tell her at the very end of the school year that we could, she and I, share the same hope even if only for a few seconds. I couldn't do that to her because she would have been too upset at the thought of having been wrong about me for so long. It often happens that I don't correct other people's ideas about me because it's simpler and I figure that everyone else does the same, even to themselves, otherwise we'd be rushed and things would change too fast around us and rapid changes tire most people, causing nausea, migraines and problems.

Well, I felt like crying. I no longer knew where to turn or how to hide. I said to myself that it was absolutely necessary to hold out until four o'clock, seeing as I was the toughest kid in the whole school and of all the students that Sister had ever taught since she started teaching in Nicolet, and from there in Yamachiche, from Yamachiche to La Tuque, from La Tuque to Macamic and from Macamic to Amos and maybe in other towns, I was the toughest, the biggest tomboy, the one with the least heart. I wasn't going to ruin my reputation in two seconds of physical and chemical weakness due to a sudden overproduction by my lachrymal glands. Whatever one says, reputations are made by how others see you. Like now, this could go all the way up to the principal of this school and it could be influential. So I clenched and unclenched my jaw, I bit my tongue, I tried to think of the last dirty joke Gerald had told me, I tried hard to find a crazy laugh, nothing.

So I lowered the top of my desk because she was coming closer, I just felt it and also I felt that given the tension in the room, there was going to be a cloudburst of words.

She was already next to my desk, I was looking up the holes of her flared-out nostrils, I sat and she stood, like a cop on the road looking down at a driver.

Our eyes met. I saw it in her eyes. The game was won because there was one thing she did not expect at all and she never ever would have imagined me doing such a thing because I really was the one with the least heart and the toughest. I knew that she would lower her eyes as soon as I did it and I did it. I cried right in her face, without letting her go with my eyes or anything, I cried and cried.

So Sister was severely punished by this move but I know that something is wrong with my mother and as far as my mother is concerned it doesn't get me anywhere to have someone punished.

A Woman

A WOMAN, STANDING IN front of the mirror above the cold fireplace, pulls the hairpins out of her hair. Her right arm folds and unfolds slowly, her fingers search the cleverly made bun that only the hairdresser down on First Avenue knows how to create.

The woman is not immersed in any profound daydream. She feels no regrets, her face isn't gentle or severe, sad or smiling.

Outside it's dark and very mild. The woman isn't thinking about that.

In a few hours, the yellow roses in the crystal vase will have faded. The woman is indifferent to this detail. This woman, a woman, has taken off her shoes. The soles of her feet feel the thickness of the red wool rug, but the woman herself doesn't feel anything at all. Not tiredness, or lassitude, or well being. One movement for each hairpin in her hair, that's all. She doesn't hear the phone ring. Or the doorbell. She doesn't hear the door opening. She isn't surprised to see a second face in the mirror, a face that isn't hers, but appears as if it had never stopped being in the mirror at the same time as hers, that seems to have been there forever, accompanying her.

29

The Parka

W HEN HE IS HUNGRY, he goes across the street to eat in the snack-bar.

This day, fog shrouds the outlines of the buildings. The streetlights look like errant floating moons.

The man puts on his parka. He goes down to the basement and sits down. In a large rocking chair he rocks. He rocks. He watches over himself without feeling anything.

The cement sweats, marking time. Once in a while the man shrugs. Nobody knows why and there is nobody there. The man lets out a small laugh. It makes no noise.

Someone comes in upstairs. The man hears. Someone turns on the radio. It's very loud, it comes all the way down to the cellar. The man slides down into his parka. Someone calls, shouts the man's name. The man buries himself, sinking deeper and deeper. Only a few hairs are left showing. The man is gone.

Upstairs someone goes out, slamming the door.

The radio is on.

At the snack-bar, someone says that there's a man who doesn't seem to be around anymore.

Marie Germain

MARIE GERMAIN ENTERED the lobby of the Queen Elizabeth Hotel. She let herself fall into the first available armchair. It was almost three o'clock on a July afternoon. Marie Germain was shaking a little. The man waiting in the armchair opposite her noticed it. At this moment he forgot what he had come to do in Montreal.

Marie Germain carefully went over her purchases and arranged them into one bag. Then she stretched for a long time as if she were at home all alone.

The man told himself that Marie Germain was not beautiful, but he forgot about the Scotch he had decided to get.

Marie Germain began to watch the people moving around in the lobby. Her eyes met the eyes of the man sitting across from her. Nothing happened, not in her eyes or in his. Marie Germain didn't think about anything. She closed her eyes. July would never end. Or August. Or any other month. She breathed deeply.

The man said nothing to himself. Marie Germain got up to drink a lemonade in the hotel café. The man followed her. At the door to the café, Marie Germain changed her mind and went straight out to Dorchester Boulevard. She shielded her eyes with her hand and walked slowly westward. Her shopping bag weighed her down. Exactly in front of the cathedral she set the bag on the sidewalk. She looked at the statues of the twelve apostles overlooking the cathedral. The man followed Marie Germain's eyes and again their eyes met, without expressing anything. Marie Germain's lips were slightly parted. The man told himself that Marie Germain must be thirsty. Marie Germain continued walking towards the park next to the cathedral without picking up the bag. The man hurried up behind her, took the bag, and not knowing how to call Marie Germain, continued to follow her.

Marie Germain checked her watch, looked surprised, hailed a taxi, and was swallowed up in it. The car disappeared in the traffic of the boulevard. The man sat down on a bench, he opened the bag hoping to find an address or a name on a bill. He found letter paper, a drawing book, felt tip pens, China ink, new cassettes, a red cotton scarf, a small jar of black olives, a marble bracelet. The marble was cool. The man held it a moment in his hand. He then remembered that he was in Montreal on business. He shrugged, got up, threw the bag into a large wire basket, and turned, going in another direction.

For A Navy Blue Sweater

I FEEL LIKE I'M in a movie. I have an appointment to make love. We'll pretend that this isn't a secret affair, yet he'll choose a motel in a direction away from his home and he'll hope all evening long that he won't meet a familiar face.

He always gets out of his huge plushy LTD to open the door for me. Silence, cameras, action! The dialogue is sparse. Things are always going well, he's always very busy, in the summer he's getting better at golf, in the winter at curling, his wife is well, his children are preparing for the good life. He gratefully answers all my questions. He does everything with gratitude. He shakes my hand with gratitude, he smiles with gratitude, he lights his cigarette with gratitude, he steps on the gas with gratitude.

"Are you hungry? Would you like to eat somewhere?"

That is always the beginning. Am I hungry? Do I need vitamins? Invariably, I answer yes, certainly, one must eat, it's necessary, in our situation there is no way around it, it cannot be done any other way.

"No, let's change our routine tonight. Let's eat afterwards."

Did I say something funny? He laughs. What am I doing here? He's got nothing going for himself. Bug eyes, balding, flat nose, no lips to speak of. Knotty rough hands.

"All right," he says with gratitude. "Shall we go to the same place? Did you like it the last time?"

"Very much."

On the contrary, I didn't like it at all. I hate motels. If his summer house wasn't so far away we could go there. Motels have no germs. It's unhealthy. Motels have no vibrations. He hasn't told me yet how beautiful I am. He'll say it at the next traffic light. It's predictable. Otherwise, he would surprise me and he certainly doesn't like surprises. He never surprises me. He always makes predictable choices, gives predictable gifts, phones at predictable times, all his ties are predictable, just like all his caresses.

"You look very beautiful tonight."

"You're so kind."

See what I mean? We are formal with each other. It makes him sweat, he doesn't quite get it, this politeness that I impose on him. It worries him. I reassure him by squeezing his hand which reassures him because it's exactly what he expects in order to be reassured. Of course, he drives an automatic, it makes holding hands easy.

He gets out. He'll rent the room. He'll come back shaking the keys. He'll whistle as he comes away from the motel office. That's it. He whistles. He parks right in front of number fourteen. Fourteen. It doesn't ring a bell with me. Can't be an anniversary. Oh yes. July fourteenth, French National Day. At least that's something. Let's enter joyfully, my brothers and sisters. I rush to open the window. I unwrap the glasses. I take all the little soaps out of their wrappers. I turn back the bed. I unfold the towels and wash-cloths, I finger everything. He laughs.

"You never forget."

He says it with admiration, with gratitude. Really, I never do forget. What could make you forget that you are about to go to bed in room fourteen, anonymous and disinfected, with an antiseptic odour that makes you want to mess it up as much as possible. While I pile my clothes on the armchair and chest, he fixes my Pernod and his rye. He has a cute portable bar, compact, discreet, well stocked.

"To the health of my wonderful mistress!"

"To the health of your wonderful mistress!"

Mistress, no kidding! What a way of looking at things. A man who turns out the lights before he takes off his pants pretends to have me, my true self, me as his mistress. I drink half of my Pernod in one shot. My head whirls. He is sitting on the edge of the bed. He will untie his laces before taking his shoes off, I know it in advance. This is not a man who would take off his shoes without untying the laces first, not him. And he will need hangers, too. What am I doing here? Can you tell me that?

"Are you coming?"

"Yes, of course."

He is sweet. He points to the bed. I am sweet. I join him. I lie down without spilling my drink. Like a good girl, I undo his tie, his buttons, his belt. I know what I'm doing, I understand him, tenderly I rub his temples, knowingly I mix mother, mistress, and little girl. Here now are the sighs, the big, letting-go sighs. Here now are the sighs, the little sighs of desire. I do everything that must be done. I am not giving him time to take me, I am taking him myself, it's less risky. I am all over him. He moans. He groans. He says oh god. He keeps his eyes closed. He doesn't dare turn off the bedside lamp anymore because each time I turn it on again since I want to see his face, his awful face hardly moved by pleasure.

"You are a wonderful mistress."

He is already up, he is already in the shower, he is already doing his sit-ups. He is already whistling while he dresses. He

43

throws me a little kiss each time he passes by the window where I am looking out into the courtyard where each car is parked in front of a door with a number.

"And you, my sweet mistress, you didn't... "

He's sincere. No, I didn't... After a few useless tries, I convinced him that just doing it was enough. He is not talented, that happens, it's no big deal. Just the same he has to protest a little.

"Ah, I will never understand women."

"I'm hungry!"

I want oysters, it's the season. A dozen fresh oysters and lemon and I want escargot with garlic and a Bordeaux, a good, expensive Bordeaux, *expensive*. Isn't it funny how all of a sudden when one needs affection the word *expensive* rings in one's mind.

"I brought you a little present from England."

"Wait, I want to guess... cookies?... no, a Wedge-wood candy dish then?... I give up."

It will be a wool sweater, I bet. It has to be, because each time he goes to England his wife and his son and his daughter and his other daughter ask for wool sweaters. It reminds me of my father who would keep turning over the long thin box before opening it and say, "It's surely not a tie, is it?"

We leave the motel forever because next time we'll nest somewhere else for a change. Change, after all, is very important in the business of love.

In the car, he turns on the radio right away. It stimulates the imagination, it bridges the lulls in the conversation. The gift is on the rear seat in a brown paper bag you understand I couldn't wrap it I hope you like it. It's a navy blue wool sweater. I try it on right then. I am thrilled. I look at this man with my eyes as full of gratitude as his. He offers me his lips.

"I would have liked to have given you much more."

"It's too much, it's much too much."

We are heading downtown. Green light. Red light. Friday evening. Traffic is still slow. I'm not hungry anymore. I just feel like lying down with my blue wool sweater. I feel like curling up forever at the place where parallels meet, leaving behind only a small shell on the red leather seat of an air-conditioned LTD with power brakes.

Two Cents

THEY UNDERSTOOD EACH other. There would be no crying. No tears. There would be no trial, no accounting. Neither one brought accusations: they understood each other.

They invited the few friends with whom they had shared their lives for nine years. The man oiled the two rifles, the woman inspected the photo and chose the place. They started walking.

Drizzle settled softly on the event. Everyone knew Mount Baldy. Everyone knew the Piperock, they knew where to go. As they got closer, their hair seemed to turn a little greyer. Very far away, a train whistled. Someone suggested that it would have been better to have gone in the direction of Envy River. The speaker stumbled over a stump and forgot his suggestion. Everyone gathered dead branches found on the way. That was part of the agreement. The man passed around the flask filled with liquor. No one refused a drink.

They knew the rites and understood the ceremony. They had been initiated to the songs of the monks at a very early age. They built up the fire until it reached new growth on the pine branches. The woman was crouching. The rifle between her legs looked like a soft old animal. As always, the man stood sideways, breathing. This assured the others that he was absent despite appearances.

When the moment came to present the offerings, the friends broke into an old song. Now you could see the dove in its white cage. Everyone was thrilled. The cage was put down near the fire and everyone was hypnotized by the flames. Stupid little things that surfaced in their minds, very ordinary things, resolved themselves, melting away in the heat. They chose not to remember anything, none of the innumerable ecstasies, none of the thresholds crossed. Nothing, by choice they were remembering nothing. In the middle of their forest, they consented absolutely to the evidence of the present.

The man and the woman aimed their rifles. They trusted each other. There was only one bullet and there was no way of knowing which weapon fired the shot that split the fog, the cage and the bird with the necklace. No one ever tried to figure it out.

They went their separate ways. They met children who were running yelling: "We heard shooting!"

They got back to their downtown offices and continued to read the same newspapers without being moved.

Much later, the man met the woman in a tobacco shop. She said she was two cents short for her pack of Camels. The man had them.

The Yellow Dress

MARC HUNG AROUND, lingering. He watched the skaters criss-crossing the channel. He didn't feel like going back to his bare room. The cold forced him to move on. He left in the direction of the campus. The streets were empty. The image of a bright yellow dress surfaced in his head. "You are sad, you are dressing sadly, you look like an anonymous being," said the dress.

Even so, the yellow dress warmed up the feeling of the street. "You will never do anything that's *colourful*."

The yellow dress faded away, mumbling. Marc shrugged, he hesitated a moment in front of the restaurant La Chandelle. Thinking about the lighting, the smells and the faces, he continued on his way. At this time, the Wasteland should be empty.

He went down the steps taking care not to bang his head on the low frame of the door. Marc wasn't one of the regulars at this small campus café. Two students, their noses in their books, and a chess amateur looking for a partner, barely lifted their heads to see who had entered.

It was a self-serve café. Marc warmed his fingers on the coffee cup, taking time to choose a table. He took off his classic dark blue coat and folded it carefully over the back of a chair, evidently conscious of creases. He tugged on the sleeves of his shirt so they extended slightly from under his ivory pullover of fine, caressing wool. Each one of these movements cost him dearly.

Marc was absorbed by a world touching on the unshapen pure, a world that drained away all of his energies leaving a kind of vacuum from which one always wanted to break out with force and violence by imposing a movement in the concrete world.

Marc took a first sip of coffee and concentrated on it as long as possible, listing the anatomical regions that the liquid passed through. Then his mind was again taken up by the invisible sponge, the absorbing parallel universe where Marc spent most of his time.

The piano next to Marc was suddenly attacked by a pianist whose aim was apparently to shatter it. The antique piano agreed to let out sounds, and then began to sing. Marc observed that the falling sound waves became still as soon as they were captured by the transforming sponge of his interior world. The pianist got angry and called out to Marc. With difficulty, Marc snapped out of his reverie, came to the surface and shifted his eyes over to the pianist.

"I can't help it," said Marc. He took his second sip of coffee without letting go of the pianist with his eyes.

"Shit!" the pianist swore.

"I would very much have loved to be a pianist like you," whispered Marc.

"I am a musician. I do not like pianists. They are sad because they have to follow the music."

The musician started to feel sympathetic towards Marc. He held out his hand over the table:

"No hard feelings. Do you like dogs?"

"I don't know," said Marc. "I know that dogs bark. They are supposed to be faithful. Someone said it could cost up to twenty-five dollars a month to keep one. I don't know."

Exhausted by all these words, Marc took a third sip of coffee.

"You are misinformed. A big dog like mine, a mix of Shepherd and Labrador, costs ten dollars a month maximum. Let's be friends."

"Hey, Mr. Pianoplayer, you want to play a game?" asked the chess amateur.

The small coffee-house filled up. Marc, glad he had arrived before the others, kept his eyes lowered so that he could avoid inviting glances that would lead to someone sitting down at his table. There are always those kinds of looks in small cafés. Marc always managed to escape them.

"Do you mind if I sit down?"

She had on a black hat that covered half of her face. She didn't wait for an answer as she unrolled a long black scarf. She put her coat on top of Marc's coat. She went to get some coffee. Marc watched her and found her almost skinny in her all black attire. She too warmed her fingers on her cup. Her eyes squinted around the room before she sat down. She took out a lighter and a pouch of Camel tobacco from an immense black bag that she had put under the table. She continued to rummage patiently in her bag until she found the Vogue cigarette paper whose yellow carton reminded Marc of the image of the bright yellow dress. He looked at his watch. Eight o'clock. He had promised to phone her at eight. He thought about it for five seconds. Then he let it go and examined the one who had taken possession of the table, the arsenal of tobacco on her left, the coffee on her right, and in front of her a small notebook that she fingered as if it were porcelain. From the bag she took out an ink bottle and pen.

She slowly unscrewed the top of the little bottle, proceeding with care like a young student. She made her pen draw up the ink, waiting until she heard the slurping noise from the ink bottle. She rolled herself a cigarette. Then she cleaned up the crumbs of tobacco that had fallen on the table. She lit up.

"OK."

She let out a long sigh in Marc's direction as if to make him witness the fact that she had accomplished precision work with which she was very satisfied. She then opened the small notebook, leaned over it and smiled. She read two pages, turned to the next ones. Her smile broadened when she saw the two white pages. She took her pen and got ready to write.

Because of the hat, Marc only saw the lips and chin of the person. A few minutes went by without any disturbance. The girl didn't write. She only moved to bring her cigarette from the ashtray to her mouth, from her mouth to the ashtray. More minutes passed. The girl lifted her head and looked at Marc with surprise.

"That's unheard of."

Marc took the last sip of coffee. It was cold but by now he was warm. The girl insisted.

"That's unheard of," she repeated.

She was most certainly addressing him. It was his turn to be surprised.

"It's surprising. Unheard of, I don't know," said Marc.

"That has never happened to me," said the girl.

"There are many things that never happen," said Marc.

"Do you do this often?" asked the girl.

"I can't help it," said Marc. "I assure you that I can't help it. It's the sponge."

"But it's rare, isn't it, a sponge like this?"

"I don't know if it's rare. It's certainly very demanding.

I'm used to it, to its hunger. Excuse me please."

"Why?"

"I don't know," whispered Marc. "I often need to excuse myself. Especially when I talk about myself."

He tried to turn the conversation around, but he couldn't master the technique. You need lots of practice to achieve this kind of a turn-around when there are not many navigators.

"I've never seen you here," said the girl.

She spoke gently, in a deep voice, and her body did not move, nor her head, or her hands. Marc appreciated this type of person because he could better make out the sense of the words.

"And what's your name?" asked Marc trying to clear his throat.

"My name is Frédérique, but it's not that simple."

"We're on a dangerous slope," said Marc with a clear voice now.

"So let's not stay here," said Frédérique.

She put everything into her bag.

"It's only two steps from here," she said rolling her scarf around her neck.

"We can take a little detour if you like. I'd like to have a little more time to get used to this idea."

The lights of Laurier Street brightened crossing King Edward and got darker after that until it became almost black. They walked down Nelson Street and came back towards the west. Frédérique pushed a door and guided Marc up some stairs. She plunged into her bag taking time to come out of it.

"I thought you weren't coming out again," said Marc. "I got worried."

While she felt around for the keyhole, the rising voices of a man and a woman were heard, one against the other. A firing of blasphemies, some insults, and a slap. Frédérique managed to open the door and turn on the lights.

"Are you used to the idea by now?"

"There are still some blunders to be avoided," said Marc.

A bright yellow dress appeared next to the chest of drawers. Marc put it on a hanger in the closet of the room. "Here we are," he said.

Green Chartreuse

LOUIS TOLD HIMSELF that soon he would be out of green Chartreuse. After hesitating for a moment in front of the piano, he chose the red swivel chair. He started to go through his weekly accumulation of journals, magazines and newspapers.

He let the phone ring long enough so he could guess who it would be. He answered in a neutral voice. The voice at the other end was cold.

"It's me. Hello."

"Hello... "

There was silence, then a great laugh that overflowed from the receiver in Louis' hand.

"That's it, you recognized me!"

Louis remained neutral, he sighed. With a slightly reproachful tone he let her know that it had been some time.

"Yes, it's been a while. I've become a stranger, that's true. Even to myself."

"Are you alone?"

"No."

Louis swivelled around in his chair. From the sixteenth floor, he could see Sherbrooke Street going east into the distance.

"So... and how are you?"

"Not good."

"No one dead, I hope," said Louis.

"Not yet."

Louis sighed.

"Should I laugh?"

"There is nothing that you *have* to do."

Her voice became small. Louis ran his fingers through his hair, then on his chest through his open shirt. He rubbed his neck. The other one sniffled, trying to get hold of herself.

"Are you crying?"

"Yes, I'm crying."

She laughed just a little. Louis noticed the weather sign over on Dorchester Boulevard announcing good weather. The other one lit up a cigarette. Her breathing became normal again.

"Come to think of it," she said, "I don't know why I'm calling you. How are you, Louis?"

"I'm OK."

"And work?"

"That's all I do."

"Love?"

"Don't have time."

"So... is that it?"

Louis was just about to whisper something gentle.

"We could go out to eat one of these days," he said.

"One of these days then... yes. See you."

Louis shrugged his shoulders and took a small sip of Chartreuse, holding it in his mouth for a moment after hanging up.

Christmas Eve

"Y<small>OU SAY THAT</small> the stores had closed their doors and that the streets were getting empty. You say that you had all the time in the world because we weren't meeting before midnight and you took your time looking at shop windows. Then you were cold. You went to the station to get warmer. You sat down at the counter and you ordered a cup of coffee. Good. All right. You say then you saw a man across from you on the other side of the counter. His head was down on the counter next to his cup of coffee. Is that it? I bet you felt sorry for him right away. No I don't bet it, I know it. So, you were concerned. Then what happened?"

". . ."

"Then he raised his head and started to look around for a sugar bowl. He couldn't find one. What about the waitress? Wasn't there a waitress?"

". . ."

"You say that the waitress didn't have time to get him one. And then? What? What did he do?"

". . ."

"You say he took the salt-shaker and put salt on everything: coffee, counter, floor, coat, pants, the inside of his pockets, all with large, sweeping gestures. OK. Why are you crying? He was drunk. OK. So what?"

" . . . "

"Listen! You are choking so much I can't understand a thing. You say that you don't want it to be Christmas because when he took out a cigarette butt from his pocket and lit it, there was a lump in your throat. Is that it? Are you telling me to stop shouting into the telephone like this? Is that it?"

"Yes, that's it, I beg you to stop shouting and repeating word for word everything I say," whimpered Bea. "So he got up and scanned the room, a pitiful look, trying to make contact with the reality of forms and he couldn't do it."

"Ah!... I see the scene. How you felt sorry for him. How your soul was torn when his eyes met yours. You read in it the despairing call of the great drowned ones of the history of the world. You wanted to fly to his rescue, to appease him, to love him, to *understand* him, right?"

"He excused himself all around. He said that he needed to step out for a minute and that he would come back. He promised us he would come back. Not to worry about him. He adjusted his spotted silk scarf, he took a few steps through all the bags, oh!... dear, large steps so as not to stumble. You know, big steps like you take in the dark when you think you are going to miss a step on the stairs or when you think the cat is there."

"Bea, can you imagine the patience it takes to listen to this unlikely story on the telephone when you really should be here with me and when I hear the champagne corks hitting the ceiling?"

"I'm sorry. Go back to them, dear."

"You say 'go back to them dear!' And here I am trying to understand why you are not coming over to keep me company. Go on."

"But I don't want to spoil your fun... "

" . . . "

"OK. So the man stopped, he caught his breath, he turned away and got to the telephone without stumbling, quite dignified. Do you understand? In a dignified way. He took an old matchbook out of the pocket of his shirt, and a dime from his pant pocket."

"An old dime, no doubt."

"Yes, an old ten cent piece, all worn down."

"You could no longer see the head on this dime."

"That's it, and he put the dime into the quarter slot and he tried to dial a number he couldn't read. It was horrible."

"And you stayed fixed on your stool, and you didn't go to help him, and you watched him turn his matchbook in all directions, I see the scene, I see it."

"I was afraid, dear, I was scared."

"Bea, it's Christmas Eve, all men are brothers. What were you afraid of?"

"..."

"Well, let *me* tell you what scared you so much. You were afraid of his appreciation. You were afraid that out of gratitude he would lift your skirt or touch your breasts. You were afraid to see your intoxicating pity disappear in the face of this beautiful drunk's breath. Tell me if I am wrong now, tell me that I am off track."

"..."

"Bea... are you there?"

"He shrugged his shoulders several times, he didn't take back his money. He turned around and he came back to the counter in the same way he had gone, picking his way through the bags. He didn't sit down. You know, he excused himself with extreme politeness for having to leave. He said that unfortunately he couldn't spend Christmas with us. He announced in a loud voice without slurring his words that this was totally unforeseen and that he was sorry not to have known earlier. He wished us a happy and a healthy New Year. And the worst, oh dear, the worst, was that he blessed us all. You get that? He blessed us."

" . . . "

"Dear? Are you still there?"

"And you wanted to adopt him, take him home, kiss him. You found, like Jesus no doubt, that he deserved it. Am I right Bea?"

"Yes dear, but I *couldn't*. It's horrible."

"And then? Go on."

"That's all, that's it. I'm not in the mood to celebrate anymore. It's too sad."

"That's it? *Bea*!... You're ridiculous. You can't ruin my Christmas Eve for a story like that, my party and all my fun?!"

"Listen my dear, I'm going to hang up, I'm ridiculous and I feel terrible and I'm angry at myself. I'm sure you can have a good time without me. If you want to yell, you can yell tomorrow when you come over, dear, please forgive me."

Bea hung up. She crawled under the covers and holding back a crazy laugh, she whispered:

"Merry Christmas, old drunk!"

The Observing Mind

T HE MAN IS SERIOUS. He puts the map of Ohio into my hands and says:

"One single mistake, and you're out. You're either a co-pilot or you're not."

Highways cross, unroll, bend into each other in circles. They are all well numbered. Deep down it doesn't matter to me if he makes me get out. I travel light.

Cleveland. It's five p.m. He chooses the motel. Makes himself at home. Takes a shower. He is tall, very hairy, very tanned. He turns on the T.V. He orders a meal through room service. Eats. Drinks his tea. Watches the tube. The news, a movie, now, he'll see me. That's it, he saw me.

"Hi," he says.

He smiles, trying to loosen up. He holds out an arm and his hand discovers my ear.

"You've got pretty ears."

I work like the tube. He knows it, he adjusts the channel to suit himself. His penis is long, thin like him but not hairy. But that doesn't matter to me either. He's careful. He says he doesn't trust women. That's why he comes on my belly. I clean it up. He is serious. He sleeps. Dreams a little. He gets up to pee. Falls asleep again. Wake up time. He shaves. Takes a shower. Dries himself. He notices that I am here.

"Good morning," he says.

He closes his luggage. Carries it to the car. I pay the bill. He puts the map of Ohio on my lap.

"One mistake, and you're out."

I make no mistakes. The airport. I get out of the car. I close the door. I board the plane. I sit down beside a businessman who drinks Scotch and reads the *Times*. He notices me. Tries to loosen up.

"Good morning," he says.

That's it. I've had it. I can't wait for the plane to take off. I tell him, sorry, I don't speak English. And the airplane takes off.

"You're kidding!... "

Not at all. The other one drives all day. At night, he chooses his motel. Takes a shower. Eats. Watches television. The news, a movie, and then he'll notice that I am not there.

The Fourth Century Chinese Gong

THE MAÎTRE D' of Pierre de Coubertin's dining room asked us to wait a moment, assuring us that a table would be free in a few minutes. He regretted that we hadn't thought of making reservations.

Dear old Isabelle sank her head in a series of excuses, explaining how we met, she and her husband, my husband and I, totally by chance, and that old friends that we were, we had decided, on the spur of the moment, just like that, spontaneously, and to tell the truth, a bit impulsively, to eat out together, taking a chance coming here without reservations and if the maître d' and the owner of this hotel and the chef would please accept us despite our unforgivable omission, we would be eternally grateful to them, nothing less than eternally grateful, dear old Isabelle.

I already saw the moment coming when Isabelle would melt into excuses to the wine steward because I would order red wine to go with the Alaskan king crab.

The maître d' listened politely to dear old Isabelle's explanations, running his worried index finger between his starched collar and his irritated neck, all the while pretending to study his reservation book.

It was obvious that the man was worried. I wanted to distract him for a moment. I said to him:

"Is it a false collar?" and I moved my eyes quickly over to

an object sitting on a liturgical shelf on a wall covered with paper exuding Oriental pretensions.

"No, Madame, that is a very old Chinese gong."

"Very, very, very old, no doubt, and I stared now at the shelf."

"It is from the fourth century."

"Was this before Jesus Christ?"

The man really looked at me now, he tried once more to stretch his collar while I filled my eyes with all that meant to say "Listen, don't make such a big deal, one, two, relax, *just feel at home*, even if we are obviously in a foreign land here, in a strange environment, wouldn't you just love a good old Blue, no, not your brand, then how about a Molson?"

Isabelle, dear old Isabelle, her husband and my husband got started in a serious conversation on Oriental art, I don't know what launched them in this direction, it seemed to me the painted paper had something to do with it.

The maître d' took a few steps towards me, considerably reduced in pomp and circumstance, said, like an accomplice, in *sotto voce:*

"Between you and me, an old gong, Chinese or not, is just an old gong, if you see what I mean."

"I'm with you, my girdle is killing me."

The man then had the sublime and vulgar audacity to bring not his index but his middle finger to the collar that was choking him, all the while staring at the carpet, oriental too but not flying, it must be said, that despite the luxury of this hotel, it was not a flying carpet. Then he turned around.

The maître d' of Pierre de Coubertin's dining room stiffened, looked over our heads and announced:

"If the ladies and gentlemen would please follow me."

Following him, I noticed that his shoes were very well polished except for one place on each heel, as if the person who polished them had put them on to do it; as if this person was not able to reach far enough to apply polish clear around the heels, or as if this person was afraid of messing up the floor on which the task had to be accomplished, not having covered the floor with a protecting newspaper. I took care not to indicate this to Isabelle. It would have been pure and simple perversion, for her and her husband and for mine, because it would have called into question the fact that the maître d' was an authority on fourth century Chinese art, and that we were getting ready to eat like the well-heeled when already Isabelle's and my husband were secretly fighting over the bill.

The Almond

Frost flowers are growing on the sides of brothels. The night is decked out with ribbons and rhythms. Men gamble at my tables for love of play and money. All my men are here—they alone. Chewing away on party-whistles, they float and mingle at different levels of resolve, feeling the lip of one or the tongue of another, depending on the disguise or the work of the mask.

Necks are damp, drink is plentiful, breath and smoke are one. A belly-up fish swims in the retinas. The flannel doll wanders towards the fireplace. Way back by the hearth the braids of the young Jew decorate the soot stuck on the useless wing.

The male king weighs his words and tries to come to terms with the presence of the others.

"You are," he says, "afraid of words, afraid that they'll catch you. You stay very far from the wonder of the archangel and you always break his rhythm. You keep the janitor in charge of the secret of the vault at a distance."

"You are," he says, "afraid of words and yet you say them, you speak the surest of them while your feet look to get a grip on the ground that fell away a long time ago. Gravity terrorizes you. To counter this, you use many allusive smiles making our party thin and tired."

"The king is losing it," murmur my chosen ones. And so as not to tell him and to remain polite, they make paper airplanes out of the pages from my books, play at amusing each other by flying them until they land in the fireplace and melt in flames.

The male king commands that I get the child and bring him here. I leave the room and enter the room of air where this child of twenty that must appear is sleeping. How beautiful he is, sleeping, wrapped only in sheets with his luminous forehead untroubled by the unanswerable question. I lift him and I carry him in my arms. He weighs no more than an armful of lilacs. His blue eyelid encloses the almond. Frost crystals quiver lightly on his lips and I bring him out.

The child wakes up. He opens his gifts. His smiling arms send out kisses. His chest distills a very fine milk. His belly is a constellation of graffiti like a wall in a men's restroom. He offers his hip lovingly as a surprise. He sweetly takes in everyone, everyone is taken in. Everyone is loosening up, everyone follows this child who signals them to follow. A strange procession falls in line with the soft step that leads a meandering parade through the house. Everyone peels off layers or gloves while a quiet morning draws the horizon and paints the heady frost flowers where grey wasps swarm.

The child finally comes to a halt before the hearth. His eyelid lets us see the almond distinctly, whose subtle perfume keeps the room in balance. Then he offers his body to the fire, first his hands, then his chest; it's quick, a newspaper catching on fire.

Everyone checks their watches. "We can't stay here like this, stupefied forever!" cries one of them in a false voice barely regained. Dragging their feet, everyone tries to find their wraps and gloves, like professional players after the fight. The male king gives thanks in the name of everyone and they leave, stepping normally, shivering in the new morning.

I get a card this morning. "My dear," it reads, "you are the queen of the illusionists and the make-up of your child was perfect. As to the trick with the fire, I give up, I won't try to understand it. I believe you are a witch. So, when will be our next get together? Fond regards, the male king."

6550

I FOUND A PARKING space just across from it. That makes things easier because things are not that simple. I stared at the 6550, wanting to find his window, but with twenty floors, you have to figure it out, count from the bottom up, he is on the sixteenth floor. The problem is that you never know if the ground floor counts as the first floor or if the first floor is called the ground floor. And then, when you count with your eyes, you're never quite sure when you miss a floor. Of course, you can always count backwards beginning with the top, but you can never tell where the twentieth floor begins, because often there is a floor with a swimming pool or a floor for machinery, you just can't be sure.

In any case, I finished my cigarette, put on my gloves, buttoned up my coat and got out of the car. I locked the car, you never know, even if I have a small car all done for and beat up, you never know, you never know anything.

It is clear that I should have phoned before coming here, right across from him. But it's not always as easy as that, a simple phone call. Because I don't necessarily always want my boyfriend to know where I am off to, because since he is my boyfriend, I'm supposed to tell him everything I do. When he is at home, even if he is sleeping, and he sleeps dead to the world, you never know, he could get up to go to the bathroom or something like that and he would hear me speaking to someone and he would ask who is on the phone. It's not that he is particularly jealous or that he wants to control me or anything like that, not at all, we're not like that, possessive and all, we two, no, he would ask out of habit, he always does. And since I believe that it would be perfectly useless for him to know Mike's name because it wouldn't mean anything to him and of course out of habit he would ask who is this and of course I would tell him no one because it really is no one to him, it would get very complicated because things are complicated and personally I like things to be simple. Even if it complicates life a little for me, that's OK, I prefer a complicated life to complicated things.

But I could have called from the phone booth at the pharmacy at the corner. True, but our janitor is always there gossiping and he is nice, he always wants to help, anything at all, he'd do it for me. And if he saw me in the process of phoning from the pharmacy at the corner, he would no doubt ask if my phone was out of order and if he could help me with anything. In the end it's more practical to make a call a little further away. So, I get in my car, it's always like that, and once in the car when I'm finally warm and my seat belt is buckled and my coat is pulled straight underneath me so as not to get wrinkled, I don't feel like getting out to make a call because then I would have to start all over again.

Anyway, I was here now. In any case, here on the sidewalk, I checked in my bag to see if I had brought along my address book because I happen to forget it more and more often and then it is a whole other story to try and remember the number of the apartment because it has four numbers. I found my book. Murray's Restaurant is just below the 6550. Great, that's good for all sorts of reasons. I got closer to the window on which there were pictures of what there is to eat in the restaurant and I looked under the letter N to see if Mike was listed there. I really should make up some rules about my address book, and stick to them because the way I enter either the family name or the first name is a waste of time. When I look for Julie's number, for example, I waste so much time. Julie's name used to be Julie Chavarie-Mathieu. Then, she got divorced. Then, she got remarried and now her name is Julie Chavarie-Bourdais. With all these changes, how do you expect me to find anything in my book.

In any case, Mike isn't under N in my book, he is under M. I held the place with my index finger so I wouldn't have to start all over again once I was in front of the huge board full of names and all, there are a lot of people at 6550.

I opened the door of 6550. I looked in my book. 1614 is the number of his apartment. I almost rang, but then I said to myself no you can't do that. I stepped back to think about it. No, it's true, you can't do that. Everyone has their private life. You can't arrive at just any hour of the day any old evening of the week at just anyone's to cry wolf even if you had what is called an intimate relationship with this someone. You never know. You could mess up your life forever with surprises like that. There are things in life that are very tricky, and life is complicated enough the way it is without me muddling in other people's lives, after all, the life of others is still a life. So I left the lobby and I passed an old couple that minced their steps on the frozen sidewalk, these old folks shouldn't have gone out in such weather, there must have been an emergency and emergencies won't wait.

So, I went into Murray's because I was sure there would be a public telephone at the back of the restaurant, or in the front. There were two public telephones in the front. Had I seen them from the street or the sidewalk I would have phoned Mike before going into 6550. It was still not too late and as luck would have it, one of the two telephones was free, the other one was occupied by an old man, there was no doubt that he was not there trying to hide anything from his wife or whatever, he just made a regular old phone call, open and all, he spoke loud but not too loud, but enough so that no one else would hear whatever I was going to say to Mike and that was fine with me. So I dialed Mike's number that I had in my hand since you know when and then I hung up real quick, before it even rang at the other end. My heart was pounding because I didn't remember what I wanted to tell him and how to say that I was here and if I should pretend that I was further away and maybe let twenty minutes or so go by between the call and ringing the bell downstairs.

To calm down a little I ordered a cup of coffee. Coffee generally makes people nervous, but with some people, it has a soothing effect, you can see this phenomenon with many people. And a brioche, it's a matter of breathing deeply and making a final decision. I told myself that he'll either be watching T.V. or puttering around. Puttering around would be everything else except watching television. And you don't know Mike, but there are only two ways for him not to get bored, this guy is really serious, it is only when he is at work at the Research Institute or when he screws that he is not bored. And when he screws, he unhooks the phone, and when he is at the Institute, he is not at home. After I thought of everything and finished my brioche, I was a little more calm. I knew that I wouldn't risk anything phoning him and if he answered at all it would be a sign that he was bored. I got up and went to dial the number from my book again.

There was an answer. It was him, it really was him, I recognized his metallic voice. He sounded surprised and when he is surprised, his voice sounds even more metallic. I asked if I was bothering him, which is what I always ask no matter what I think. He answered that I wasn't bothering him in the least, that he was actually bored watching T.V. and he asked where I was and where I was phoning from, and all. I said I was home, which was a lie, I couldn't help it, had I told him I was downstairs he would have felt obliged to invite me up and if there is one thing that I don't want to do it's to force myself on someone, I can't do that. I have not yet analyzed this part of my personality but I will get to it one day, one always does.

Mike asked if I wanted to come over. He didn't ask me to come over, he asked me *if*. In other words, he didn't want to get involved in the decision of whether or not I would come over. Mike is like that, he doesn't like to influence people. He doesn't say that he would like that or love it or that he needed to. That would compromise his independence, it's a kind of principle he always follows, and there is no way he'll change because he has always been like that and he doesn't like to try different principles in general because he believes that you have to have good reasons to change your principles, especially when it begins to affect the independence of an individual with an average lifespan of sixty years.

I knew about that personal trait of Mike's. That doesn't mean that I wasn't affected by it, or that it didn't bother me at all, on the contrary. But I pretended not to notice. I pretend not to notice many things, it's a way of simplifying.

At that moment, I imagined myself up there. I saw Mike groping through my coat because we would have to get turned on quickly because we wouldn't have much time considering that Mike needs several hours of sleep, sound sleep, because he needs his rest for his work at the Research Institute since research must be done with a rested mind, that's what he told me.

"Are you coming or not?"

This kind of question is very clear. It's not very inviting, in my opinion. I've discussed this already with others. With Pierre, for example. Pierre thought that this was as inviting as any other way of saying it.

A large grey overcoat started to dial a number next to me. I don't know why the sight of the grey and inert overcoat dialing a number affected me, in any case, I told Mike that I was calling him on the spur of the moment, just to hear his voice, because it was so cold outside and I felt lonely, but in reality, I had no intention of going out, that's what I said. He said that we should get together some other time then. We wished each other good-night with voices full of double meanings remembering what it was like when we slept together and that it would be good if we could do it again sometime when it was convenient. The sometime, that is the blessing of this type of relationship that I have with certain professionals.

I ran to my car, the wind was gripping me from every side. I closed my door, I even locked it so the wind would stay locked out and I'd be inside. I started the car and turned on the heater. When it was warm enough, I unbuttoned my coat. I didn't feel like going home. I saw the traffic lights, I counted them. I waited to feel like going home. I was protected from the wind. My gas tank was still full. I had all the time, all the time in the world, really I did.

Scampi

HE WAS ALWAYS a good-looking man, I found him handsome right away with his cheeky, ironic look, his very red tongue, and his constant mocking lips. For the past eight years chance had it that we never found each other alone, I always with a lover, he always with this or that woman, brushing by each other only behind the scenes or on stage while playing a role.

"What will you have?" he asks.

"You choose."

I hate choosing especially when I am the guest. After all, it's not I who will pay and how can I know how much to spend when someone else is paying.

"Scampi?"

I don't know. I don't remember what they taste like. And he puts his lips right under my nose, so how could I possibly remember what scampi taste like with these lips here, teasing and juicy, waiter, serve them to me.

"Scampi... scampi... yes, scampi!"

He orders scampi. White wine, red wine? It does not matter, I don't care, my words are tied up in his tongue. He decides:

"Rosé then."

He is more handsome than ever, he is wearing a shirt of

white Indian cotton with eggshell pants. He is tanned, the night is hot. He was not free before midnight, the restaurant is empty.

"You look gorgeous."

This makes him laugh, and this makes happy people come into the restaurant. Blue eyes, infinitely blue, and mocking. His mouth, a face by itself, you should have seen him in the role as mayor, a long time ago, in another street, in another town.

"You're gorgeous and a little too much."

He thinks this is funny too. He looks at me from all angles. He will end up asking the waiter to move the light to see me better. He leans over to me, no kidding, there is black in the blue. I start to notice his hands, dark, nervous, with nails trimmed short.

"They are cold."

"What?"

"The scampi."

"I'm sorry."

He makes a clown face. The mouth is a sad square. A teardrop leaves the eye and wets the red carpet after having rolled off the leather bench. Our hair is touching, our laughs embrace, it surprises us. We tell ourselves not so fast, after all, there is no hurry. He leans back and rearranges his napkin with theatrical know-how. I will never get to the scampi. What an idea, scampi at one o'clock in the morning, across from these white teeth on parade, flashing. He teases, he gets impatient, kisses me, rosé, no, I am not thirsty anymore. The waiter prepares the bill with a knowing look. If he is like me, he must have seen others like us.

We are now on the hot sidewalk, lost to our senses. His eye is so close it's as blue as the sky at mid-day. There is a crack in the iris, gee, I had never noticed this fissure in the porcelain eye, could it break, could I get hit by sparks, am I risking something? All of a sudden, there are too many people in the hot downtown night, I can't breathe.

That's it, I need air, he is sticking to me, and it smells of gasoline from Texaco and motor oil. The soles of my feet burn on the leather of my sandals and his hands implore my head, he whispers something in my ear, a car passes and covers the whisper. He clears his throat, he does.

Yes, it's true, fate wants us at last. But this chance is so hot that I am slowly evaporating. I'll end up looking like a terrible teaser, and that's not good, you should never do things like that, you just shouldn't, guys in general and girls in particular don't like it, it's against professional ethics. And this isn't the first time this has happened to me, I should have looked at this more closely to at least know what to say, to at least address this in a rational manner, to see what I want to say. He says I'm wavering, he's right, after all he was the one who put out for scampi, I agree. On the other hand it's very late and I'm slipping from him despite myself. The sun will rise, and a tiny little morning mist drifts on the canal or is it the vision of me evaporating. It doesn't matter, it doesn't hurt. It's OK. It makes me feel good.

Brief Encounter
(Without Rachmaninoff)

I HADN'T NOTICED IN the airplane and now I am curious. He has cat's eyes. When he speaks, his face hardly moves. No one was waiting for him either. We decided to come up here for a drink, both tired from jet lag. I could very well spend the night here watching the lights move on the runway.

He asked if we should take a room at the Hilton since neither of us had anyone. He told me that he thought I was beautiful, very beautiful. He doesn't know if the bar closes, or when, and neither of us really feels like asking the waiter.

I tell myself that I feel like never moving again and that someone ought to carry me to a taxi.

"Did you have a good trip?"

"Lille was very beautiful. I went to the museum."

He put his arm around my shoulders. It feels good. An airplane takes off. I'll spend the rest of my life here, I don't ever want to leave. His hands are surprising, I didn't expect this, they are like a cat with retracted claws. It's hot around my neck. He whispers questions into my ears, mostly to make my ears hot, to caress.

"Why France?"

"I had a meeting."

"Love?"

"There were many people."

His hand wanders around my back. Taking a small sip of Courvoisier creates so much heat that another airplane takes off from the runway.

"Are you thinking about the trip?"

It tickles my ear, I'd like to fall asleep like this. It rocks me. I'll spin a small cocoon for myself and doze off.

"Are you living by yourself?"

I never know ahead of time if I live by myself. Sometimes there has been someone else and I think that it could happen again, that he could come back. Since he never really definitively gave me back the keys and if he hasn't lost them, I can't be certain that I live by myself.

"I never quite know ahead of time."

His hand stopped moving. I was wishing he would think of my neck before we went home. I know that I'll have to get home. Sooner or later you have to go home. I'll collect myself and go home.

"I have to go home."

"I can take you home."

There is no luggage. We can just float across the airport. We pass in front of the boutiques where I usually amuse myself when I'm all alone before departures. My eyes close all by themselves. We are doing fine.

"The Hilton would be all right."

Yes, we would be all right. He keeps his hand on my shoulders and we go down and outside. A little wind moves over my face just the way I like it. We get into a taxi. I'll fall asleep because he is kissing my forehead and because everything is warm and touches me. Côte de Liesse, Décarie,

Queen Mary, I know where I am. I don't feel like getting out of the taxi that smells of bad air-fresheners.

Everything is left to chance, chance can accomplish many things, it has that reputation. He kisses me lightly on the mouth and already I'm on a sidewalk that perhaps follows all the sidewalks of other towns in other continents.

I go up the stairs recognizing the shape of the ramp. My keys are at the bottom of my bag as usual. I walk into the apartment, turn on the overhead light, I put down my bag and walk around to all the rooms to check the shape of the beds in the two bedrooms. No, I live alone. Yes, I live by myself.

Rich For One Day

ALINE DECIDED TO open her eyes. She had no idea of the time but by the sounds in the house that came down into her small room in the basement, she knew that just about everyone was well into their day. The theme music of Phil Donahue made its way through the ceiling, four o'clock. Aline grunted with pleasure. Was there anyone else like her who just woke up and for whom four o'clock meant only a delicious nest under a thick white sheepskin, it was most unlikely and Aline felt her good mood grow, she was incredibly lucky, and she took pity on the rest of the world.

Propping herself up on one elbow, she looked around her room. There were lots of crayons, paint bottles of all colours, notebooks, sheets here and there, and photographs, piles of photographs on the large yellow piece of plywood that she had made into a work table. Aline laughed sweetly and scolded herself that she should get serious, that the mess on the table ordered her to hours of work and that one must work to live. She sighed and she laughed and she hid her laughter in her warm pillow. How sweet it is.

Then she remembered, she was rich today. She had eight dollars, a fortune. She could allow herself thousands of things. Sitting up in her bed, she stretched her arms towards the ceiling; acknowledging her hands, she yawned with relish.

She pulled her old worn cords and loosely knit sweater towards her and put them on under the sheets to stay warm. She got up.

It was wonderful. She could go to the movies and have popcorn and Coke. The telephone rang, it was Lucien, all excited, he offered her a contract. A designer needed a photographer for his spring collection, would Aline be interested?

"You," said Lucien, "are you sleeping or are you listening?"

Aline told him that she was listening very carefully but that she was not quite awake and that she felt too rich today to give an answer. Lucien sighed, he explained to Aline that she would never be successful if she insisted on not taking things seriously, not jumping at opportunities when they came her way. Aline answered that she agreed totally with Lucien's opinion and that she often berated herself for this flagrant lack of maturity on her part, but that she really just got up and that she couldn't help it, and if he could call back... Lucien hung up and Aline put on the *Deep Purple* record already out of its jacket.

It was risky to open the black burlap curtains that held out the light. The sky could be too bright, it could be too much, Aline was careful, she preferred to take the sky outside all at once, not here in this basement. She turned on her work light and poured a glass of orange juice. She kept only orange juice in her room. Usually her friends invited her to eat with them. She wasn't difficult, whatever you say. She examined some of the negatives lying on the table, they could wait. Last Saturday's paper was open to the entertainment page, but Aline preferred to submit herself to the good taste of the schedulers at the Cinéma Outremont, expecting a surprise, she would go there and take her chances. It may be easy to find her capricious, but difficult she was not, she said to herself.

She put on her boots and looked everywhere for her keys. She wrapped herself up warmly and climbed the stairs. The street was full of people hurrying to get home, people who had finished their day, their Thursday. It was their duty to fill each day from morning to evening and to think of her day as perfectly empty; Aline felt like converting the whole world to her style of living. She got to Côte-des-Neiges.

The air was humid, the sidewalks were banked by dirty snow, a swollen sky rolled from one roof to another. Aline felt invulnerable, she was absorbed by a small stubborn happiness that warmed her from inside and her small happy steps carried her from one storefront to the next. The shop window of Renaud-Bray Books was an old friend of Aline's, always full of new items. Aline decided to go in and browse.

She opened the fat books and fingered them, she caressed and congratulated them. Books were thousands of little heaters, Aline's hands were warm and she felt good. There were other customers, they also moved from one universe to the other with the pages they turned and that made pockets of heat, no doubt about it, Aline thought to herself. It didn't occur to her to buy anything. For years now she has been in the habit of enjoying things that were available to her without feeling like she had to buy them. She didn't need anything.

To get to the movies, she would have to take two buses, the 165 and the 160. The 165 stop was just by the bookstore but there was a line and the first bus, packed, went by without stopping. Aline walked to the next stop at the corner of

Lacombe. In her oversized coat and her scarf that was too long, she felt loved and fulfilled, another bus arrived, she let it pass and continued on to the next stop across from the liquor store at the corner of Edouard Montpetit. She didn't really feel like taking a bus. She said to herself that when she was grown up, she would be very, very rich, and that she would have a car and a chauffeur, and that she would have the whole back seat to herself, and that she would be surrounded by very rare things, very beautiful things, and very astonishing things, and she would never cease being astonished at all these things around her. And she would travel, she would spend all her time in this car, and she would stroll over the whole world and not just one or two sidewalks. Because the light is too harsh in busses, Aline didn't like them. There is not much that Aline didn't like and she walked on to the next stop.

It started to snow and Aline hailed a taxi. She said to herself, "This is the way to live," she had the whole back seat all to herself, and the chauffeur drove where Aline wanted to go.

Then she settled herself in a seat at the movies and enjoyed the arrival of other people that came in with hands full of popcorn, gloves, mittens, hats and scarves. The lights went out and Aline started to eat her popcorn. The first image lit up the screen. I love life, thought Aline.

The Lavoie Woman

THE THIN NEEDLE of dream had slipped into his eye. He had been blind ever since then and never could finish the hem of his coat.

Now, he rang doorbells, he showed his certificate with one hand and reached out with the other, his cane leaning on the doorframe of the houses.

No one had rung at the door of the Lavoie woman since the last visit of the Social Welfare inspector. The Lavoie woman deemed the blind man presentable and she made him sit down to get a better look at him. She watched him for several days, lodging and feeding him, and several nights without seeing him any better. Finally, the blind man expressed a wish.

"I remember," he said to the Lavoie woman, "the light, and I have stopped believing in it. But I would like you to give me an honest description of your image with all the details of a photographic print."

After hours and hours, and these hours collapsed into the time on the clocks of the subway stations where other people were going towards other stories, the Lavoie woman answered.

"You'll have to help me," she answered, "because I can't get used to the idea that light needs faith or belief to exist."

The blind man sighed softly and continuing to slide his cane in the hollow of his hand, he explained.

"For once," he explained, "invent yourself. Here is your chance. I will not come back."

The Lavoie woman gave herself lots of time. She couldn't stop watching the blind man, she found him more and more real and of great beauty. She couldn't accept not to see herself in him. Time dissipated the surprise, the mute astonishment, and the Lavoie woman announced the news to the blind man.

"You will heal," she said. "I have consulted with experts. All you need is a small operation to get your sight back."

And as the sun rolled over the thick pile carpet of the living room, the Lavoie woman, whose chest had expanded with self-satisfaction, moved closer to the blind man to woo him even more. Her body overflowed with the joy of redemption.

"I have the address," she whispered, "we'll go there tomorrow."

The rest of the day went by quickly for the Lavoie widow, because she knew that soon she would see herself and she began to array herself. She sorted out old and new habits.

The blind man continued to think, chewing the licorice sticks that the woman had given him. He said:

"Then I'll finally see you go through the walls. Right? I know you do that well. This is what I look forward to seeing the most."

The Lavoie woman did not sleep that night. She mulled it over and changed her mind. She did not take the blind man to the appointment with the expert. When several years later the blind man again took up the road of his quest, the Lavoie woman spent many hours thinking about that period in her life when she passed through the thickest walls with no trouble at all.

Life, After All

"You say *perambulator*. You do not say *baby buggy*."
　　　　　　　　　　　　　　　　—Jachar

"You do not say *cover*. You say *blanket*."
　　　　　　　　　　　　　　　　—Jachar

I HAD TO THINK quickly. I saved the old black baby buggy. I threw newspapers into it, old newspapers and newspapers that were stuck to the curbs of the streets. When I saw it coming, I knew I wouldn't have much time. It all went through my head very quickly. You had to think fast. Know what was important. Without having to decide I held on to nothing. When it came right down to it, the decision came all by itself, I held on to it tight, I left.

The baby buggy was out there, I pushed it, I dragged it. Or was it the baby buggy that pushed, pulled, and dragged, I don't know, never knew, don't remember. Often you can't tell whether the ends of your fingers are where things begin, or if the things themselves are the beginnings of your fingers. There are fewer things here now. Now, things are simpler. There is only the little old baby buggy and inside that, newspapers, and inside them the weather reports and new news; I always knew that news is continually new, and didn't really need confirmation. Why bother, I equate it with the weather report. I alternate good weather with bad weather, creating a balance.

So, here we are. The fault engulfed it all. All this time we had lived on top like owners. The edge is a lot farther back now. There are some who went back with it, they started over again. As for me, I left.

It's a pretty solid one. Even though the wheels appear to be fine and delicate, they should last. It pulls me along. We take turns pulling, it's the best solution, since it wasn't possible to know anymore who pulled, who pushed. I didn't know if I should be grateful, if it was right that it was always the buggy that worked and never me, or always me and never it. I mark an X so that we don't get mixed up. I put an X in the margins of the paper, so that I can keep track of the turns. I make a cross with the nail of my left thumb, the one that is the longest of my ten nails. I keep it sharper than the others; it helps me to know who worked the evening before, who will work tomorrow and who is working at the moment. In my daydreams, I could very well make predictions, in order to know who would be working ninety-three days from tomorrow, or in going the other way, who worked ninety-three days ago counting from yesterday. This way there is a built-in future in this story.

We're all alone. We settled in far from the edge, and took it from there.

In the paper dated March thirteenth, it says Stravinsky's widow burned her love letters for personal reasons. Did she foresee the receding of the edges? Either she must have been swallowed up, or she left, at her age, and she did not have to think yes or no was she going to take these letters, since according to the paper they had been burned. As for myself, the letters quickly crossed my mind because it was necessary to hurry and not being used to catastrophes, it was strange to have to hurry so. But no, not the letters. The buggy only. It's all black. Its roof is torn. The newspapers are inside. Everyone really takes a turn here, we agree on this without formalities because there are fewer people than before. Before we needed contracts if we agreed to take turns and raise our hands. Here I don't raise my hand anymore, the right one naturally, never, no need anymore.

I was all dressed because I had been sleeping with my clothes on for a long time. Still, at another time I used to sleep naked. At that time there was another skin. You used them to cover up, and with time, we needed to make a collective agreement because we didn't know anymore who was covering whom and who got warmed up. And because certain skins were cold-blooded, the purchase of thermometers helped to make the agreements fair according to the temperature of the skins, and so everyone could sleep in peace. Often we suffered from insomnia despite the clarity of the law, so I started to wear a sweater, then I kept on my panties; after that I kept on my big wool plaid shirt with the blue squares. After that, I kept on my red flannel skirt, and the other skin, each one having its own, could continue sleeping naked. We didn't really pay attention any longer to the laws of the night ritual.

As I said, I was already dressed and left very quickly without taking the time to consider if I should alert the skin that slept without insomnia. I think that that skin was swallowed up, I have no news. News doesn't exist anymore where I am and where we go, both of us, me and my buggy, we have only old news to digest and that turns out to be eternal. The news from before, we feed on from time to time and we don't miss news from after since it's eternal.

But what we missed in the beginning was tobacco. It was lucky that in the beginning and even still today we reeked of it. I would never wash the buggy with its torn hood or me and my shirt. We pretend to smoke by smelling the parts that reek the most, it's a good way to save. So much for what's missing, the craving comes in the evening with the ringing of the vespers and with the taste of red wine; it's crazy but it's in the memory banks and they can to go off at the most unexpected times. You can't second-guess your memory. Almost without reason, it unwinds itself anyway. You stick your nose into the shirt and fall asleep like this, the shirt then becomes a sleeping pill. So you are careful never to wash it, it would be a total disaster, like the disaster of the edges receding, rather total.

I got rid of the brown stone. Back then I kept it in the big pocket of my flannel skirt. It would make me dream, and then it would wake me up if necessary. I imagine that I wouldn't be needing it anymore except to stimulate certain memories. The only thing left for it to do was to wake me up in the night from an uncomfortable position. I could have thrown it into my buggy, but what's the use. If you agree that everything must have a use, then everything must take its turn when its turn comes up. Looks like repetition, but not because we're settling in. We are settling in far from the edge. And took it from there.

Chances of going around in circles are great. We should mark the bark. That would give rise to the problem of traces. Do we want or do we not want to leave traces. Before, the question was what sort of traces. As a result of the different marks, there were jobs created at the Ministry of Traces. The skins discussed the marks and when it was applicable, declared them "traces." Signposts were put up at certain marks that had been declared traces, and you didn't bother with others to avoid administrative hassles. Not everyone could be a troublemaker, after all. It took hundreds of years in the offices. Luckily I was not assigned to the offices nor did the offices summon me. Just once, I was assigned to the subject of which I have already spoken, the skins and who would make whom warm. You had to go into an office, by that time I had been sleeping in my skirt for a long time, but still I had to be summoned. No, we decided to take the risk of going in circles rather than leaving marks that might possibly serve as traces for a newcomer. There is only the same old news and raw roots are edible. Of course we thought of cooking our roots, but we remembered that fires leave traces, marks, circles, indentations, wounds on wood, and so, no, no fires, only raw food, it's important if you want to eat.

It must be said that we have used a lot of our newspapers since our run for life. First, we gave up the top of the pages, all the tops. Now our news have no more dates, it's the dates on news that make them so immortal. So much was used up already, but it was necessary because they were needed. Really. My bodily functions continue as before, a little less, considering the rarity now of the old feast days, but still I want to continue to wipe myself as if nothing has happened, the little drops, and the little hole, so that it continues to stay pink, I keep to that because of pride, and also, I continue to menstruate but my skirt is red so even if I spotted, because of economic considerations, it would hardly be noticeable. Difficult to get rid of all old habits, or new ones.

Because we needed to sacrifice parts of the newspapers, there are no more dates, as I said, or names, or information as to where they came from. In any case, we're not good with names, or dates, or places; I remember March thirteenth because of Stravinsky's widow, it struck me simply because of the word "love," to burn love letters; I think this is timely news for widows, and that's the reason why it struck me.

No monkeys in sight. But lasting existence through us, black buggy and me, red skirt and blue shirt with big empty pockets loose on my breast, monkeys seen and loved long ago on the edges; impossible to get rid of the images from those times, impossible to erase the images of big monkeys with flowering hemorrhoids even after all these days, all these nights, of examining and deciphering the roots.

I have someone to talk to. I remember that this used to be a problem on the edge; skins tried to find someone to talk to, it was called despair, nothing eternal, just historical. Me too, I often looked for addresses, the ones I had never seemed enough, it was a real problem, especially on hot nights. The other skin said that at least I could take off my constant skirt despite my resolutions. There must have been some connection. But even when entertaining the idea of a relationship, I did not like to go against my resolutions. It was one of the ways of distinguishing myself for myself, without egotism or anything. It's perhaps this character streak that allowed me to escape looking like an old black buggy.

I have been worried ever since this morning. I feel that we are being followed. I don't know exactly what I saw that triggered this intuition. With me intuition always comes from something that I notice without being conscious that I noticed it. It's been awhile since I have worried, because the roots take up all my time, I no longer remember how to wrinkle my forehead to worry productively. I remember everything had to be efficient, it was of foremost importance before the edges fell in on us and their receding or their advancing, you never know.

You say perambulator, you don't say baby buggy. Never heard this statement again since my departure. Resolution: never name a root. Enough to know whether they're edible or not, that's plenty. No christening is called for. There is no need to debate on the subject of pram or buggy. Good riddance.

It's a pretty solid one. It has a fine suspension. We rest in natural trenches. Before, there was absolutely no agreement on how to determine what was natural and what was not. Since the catastrophe an agreement came about, easily. I have a natural aptitude for getting along with myself and this simplifies discussions. That was one of the reasons why I was summoned to the office. It took me awhile. Days and nights followed each other, like now, but with time, back then, they became heaps, whereas now, there are no more heaps even in their succession. And I took no stance concerning what was natural. I looked. I thought about it. The most difficult was vinyl. Vinyl posed a special problem because it did not have pores. I slept once with a skin without pores. Lying down, it's not comfortable when you have to resort to a microscope to find the pores at night. It continued to trouble me even afterwards, long afterwards, this absence of pores on the photos left behind by that skin.

Heaps of cigarette butts, too, and all sorts of pots in the bottom of cupboards, earthenware pots, glass pots, porcelain pots, terra cotta pots, pots without necks, with necks and all, it stays in your head long afterwards, but it doesn't bring up the question any longer of what is natural like it did before, each time I opened the door. How we got there, was the question. In front of any pile, the question was how we got there. Heaps, how did these heaps of things get there? All these variations on heaps and the wind had nothing to do with it, even though we don't really know if the wind had nothing to do with it, it is like my memory of the big monkeys, even if we are farther away now, very far, I am afraid that we are very near, considering the possibility of going in circles and that before there were also skins determined not to go around in circles, at least in the imagination of the river population.

That's resolved now. Everything is natural, with or without, the concern is simply not in the pores. It's the question that's not natural. It was just that you often got bored on the edge and that you knew how to invent things without wind, without grain, without sperm, without heart or anything, neither tail nor head, you often called it pleasure, or somewhere else metaphysics, depending on the different vocabularies from one heap to the next. Different vocabularies come from heaps, that's all. Now, it's all so much clearer and buggy and me, we get by pretty well with edible roots.

Perhaps the feeling of being followed comes from a dream. I thought I saw a bird. Were we still asleep in a trench, buggy, sleeping on the side, with the wind making the two wheels spin as if there was something to be milled? Did I sleep? It's difficult to admit to a bird, with everything being cut, except for the roots. Not a dove, it would all begin again, I don't want it to be a dove. Invariably there would be someone waving a white flag, and then, it's possible, if I saw a bird, that we would be followed by a skin waving a white flag, or if he was by himself, without a flag, he would be animated with his white hand as a replacement for the flag. For me, no, never again a white hand or a dove or an olive branch, all that was the same shitty vocabulary, and we took it from there.

Some sky is still left. A sliver. A bit of a cover. A bit of blue. All around it is the void, the nothing. It did seduce me when I saw that we were going to live like that, with just a sliver of the sky and everything else all black. Because of the cover it made for us and that travelled overhead with us, I was stuck, like that, like in a trance. It took some time. I stayed there for a long time not quite believing it and I said to buggy that I was on a sit-down strike, despite the fact that we were far from the heaps because of the catastrophe and all, and despite the fact that we left everything behind to be swallowed up in the fall of the edges.

Astonished. No recall of order and efficiency. No need to keep track of the input and output of participation. No shitty masses. Astonished, this cover and nothing else, roots and bark. Buggy. Red skirt is holding up pretty well, and the shirt and the empty pockets loose on my two breasts. Newspapers for news. A little more and you would have too much. As it is, this absence of belonging to a heap, this sensation blew me away. I keep thinking about it, experiencing it, I recall the smell of lavender; but here, it's better still, it's above and beyond everything.

Dreamt about the label of Chablis-Moreau. It still is sticking to the top of my neck. Pleasure: the sky lost its horizons. Horizons, before, eternal subject, created aims, ideals because of the symbols implied in the contact with nature. No more horizon. Just a cover big enough for the eye, without going overboard; before the sky was always going too far, you could never take it in all in one look. It created impressions of solitude and it created nearly all of philosophy, always trying to take in the sky in one go; this problem filled libraries to the roof. With the edges swallowed up, we go without news, the skirt is holding up, we go barefoot, we get scabby, it's OK.

Nothing new in terms of news, easy to forget them with time. Generally, news isn't sticky, that's what makes it so eternal. Only Stravinsky's widow makes me think; her story was really temporal in the sense that it continuously stuck to my skin, starting up thoughts from there. Had to sacrifice several entire pages. They had been rotting in the bottom of buggy and started to include buggy in their decomposition. I didn't think that old newspapers could rot like that by themselves; I found out. Oiled our wheels with earwax, it was all there was. Will see how it holds up and whether this will fix the slight squeak.

Found a new root. Pink. Careful. I'm making some tests. It's pink inside and outside, milky, flexible like licorice. There are no rats here to use in experiments. It smells. Reminds me of the smell of one of the skins from before on the edges. Neither salty nor peppery. Sea-like without salt. Often it was vice without the versa. Often, it was versa without the vice. When vice and versa came together, I tried again to go naked at night. But in the end, I abstained and my skirt stayed on again. The suspicion that I carry around on the subject of the pink root poisons I think the motion and the luminous blue of the cover above.

Today, the thought of flying on the edge keeps me entertained. It is perhaps the smell of the root that triggers the memory of highs. Put the root into the buggy to see if the thought of ecstasy would leave me, it's difficult, I would prefer it would not. Especially the thought of this one single time, in a city on edge and a night in July, two skins, one on the right, one on the left, almost not touching the sidewalk, desire, ecstasy and hair and the hot night, staying up, that was it, especially not going to bed, because going to bed would be to renounce the balance of the high, a rose in the mouth and a bunch of greens yanked from the gardens of a big hotel. I won't forget the balance was kept; I don't know what was saved, but balance just for balance was a rare pleasure, in its time, in the flights on the edge. After that, dawns which most people never saw unless reflected from a subway window, under the bark.

Other advantage: I deal straight. No exile or waiting room. No leftovers, nothing to recycle or to fix in formaldehyde. You don't have to make yourself understood. There is only buggy that pulls me, and me pulling buggy when it's my turn. I am in charge of the roots, I find this fair because it's impossible to do otherwise.

For music, I have words. It's soothing. Today I played Ribambella. It's OK. I change music as needed, but sometimes before going to sleep, I play something that I particularly like; there are two or three that I like best, I can say I like Ribambella very much; then, it's Tattoo, which is full of the best of sensations. Tattoo, before or when I suffer a bit because of the scabs, is best.

I am followed. I told buggy that and I said to buggy that I should carry it because wheels leave marks on bark despite the fact that we had decided not to leave marks because of the traces. I am forced to change my decision, which is not difficult, seeing that there isn't a single skin around who could reproach me for the change of heart like before on the edges where it was not seen in a good light, disapproved of, yes, to change a decision, whatever one says and despite the analyses. So, buggy on my back to avoid markings.

Painful scabs on the knees because I often am down on my knees to search for roots. It's OK. No use for this back, this surface that sometimes should come and take the place of the skin of the feet or of the knees, but it's fixed and alone back there. That's it, it's my back, that's what's following me. Discovered that yesterday evening when I slept on it and when intuition stopped. I should have thought of it; never sleeping on your back makes you forget it and it becomes another part altogether.

Days, nights, roots. Still not made a decision about the pink root in the buggy that I see each time I take an old newspaper to get up to date with news. I am happy though to be the only one to experience a new thing about which no one around me speaks, seeing that I am alone. It makes me laugh. A laugh that is absolutely mine that flutters around in my mouth like tiny black flies on the bananas from before. Am I obsessed by the pink root. My mistrust is not asleep. Going over the old story again of the skin's erection. Skins did not like to be surprised in the state of a hard-on, there was a need for conditions, the time and place had to be right, so that skins felt OK morally, otherwise, you didn't live right. Once in a while a shaking of a bus started it, and the skins perspired a little. I liked that. Never understood why not. Why not let the tongue go towards the mouth towards the tongue and everywhere on other skins since you did not risk to turn in circles on the edges considering the paid controllers. But it was the question of honour that was important and it won against the sublime.

The pink root makes me more and more uncomfortable.

Option: get rid of it, let's not talk about it anymore. If you find another one like it, just pretend not to see it and you will be OK. It's not shaped like a thorn, even though, little by little, in my head it's taking on the shape of a thorn, well, well.

I was walking with buggy on my back even though we are not being followed, buggy got used to it and likes it and this way my back can serve and not live any longer behind me completely apart, so, I was walking with buggy, when one of its wheels fell off. No use to tell stories or to invent cataplasms or stories of knots made with wheels, no, not here, we are without news. Except the news which really are eternal here, they stick less and less, difficult to make them come even to the retina. Fog.

Good riddance, good-bye and all, to the pink root today. Thrown behind my back. Asked my back to watch over it as long as it could feel it lying in the distance. That's the end of the pink threat story.

With only three wheels, buggy is almost always on my back. I don't know if I could tell its age now. Mine has no use here whereas before it had purchase power attached to it. The cover is still luminous. Blue. Stretch of sky too big before, now I would like the form to undo itself, but it's fixed, enraptured.

My hair is falling out. I had to go back to make sure that no tufts of hair had left markings. No. It's recent, from today.

The cover cleared and there was hair on the bark. I compared the loose hair to the ones on top. Same colour. It's my hair. My root diet is perhaps not balanced.

Turn the back to the light, try to change the room without packing all my luggage, for example, get close to the music without towing in the tobacco, the wine and the ashtrays, that is the advantage here. Come to think that my skirt is a soft bone that started to grow from the waist.

I played Tattoo last night, full moon in the cover above. Tears welled up in my eyes. Enough to water the lemon tree also swallowed up in the receding of the edges no doubt. I lifted up my skirt. I slept with my head on my knees. This morning my eyelids stuck together a bit. Short impression that I could not take in all the cover in one go. Memory of crazy women from before on the edges. Finally, in the end, they were parked in heaps. That way the confusion that risked to bring us closer to chaos, that risked to wake the fear of big monkeys so far but maybe so close, was avoided.

Here, the question to go forth and multiply is resolved, good riddance. No need here to contemplate obstacles to feel unified. The son of Abraham may well go on to devour his heritage.

Today, little taste on the tongue. Felt my breasts under my blue loose shirt, no bad bumps and it's still there, the same happiness at the two ends. Broke the nail on my left thumb.

Gave up on crosses in the margins. Let go of a traceable future or past. Buggy definitively anchored on my back. Knees scabby. Inevitable four-legged position.

. . .

There is life, after all. I thought as much. Others are no doubt fishing from where we are absent.

About the Translator

Susanna Finnell received her doctorate from the University of British Columbia in French Canadian Literature. She is on the faculty of Washington State University and lives in a grain elevator in Eastern Washington.

Press Gang Publishers is a feminist collective committed to publishing works by women who are often made invisible and whose voices go unheard.

For a free listing of our books in print, write to:

Press Gang Publishers
603 Powell Street
Vancouver, B.C.   V6A 1H2   Canada